Mary McLean and the St. Patrick's Day Parade

By STEVEN KROLL

Illustrated by MICHAEL DOOLING

SCHOLASTIC INC.

New York   Toronto   London   Auckland   Sydney

ISBN 0-590-43702-X

Text copyright © 1991 by Steven Kroll.

Illustrations copyright © 1991 by Michael Dooling.

All rights reserved. Published by Scholastic Inc.

12 11 10 9 8 7 6 5 4 3 2 1   2   2 3 4 5 6 7/9

Printed in the U.S.A.   08

MARY MCLEAN'S father was a potato farmer in Ireland. When the crop began to fail year after year, when the potatoes came up out of the ground healthy and almost at once turned black and rotten, the McLeans had to give up their little thatched hut in Donegal.

In the fall of 1849, Mary, her parents, her older brother Danny, and her baby sister Meghan packed what they could and sailed to America. The ship was big and wide, but traveling steerage, they were tightly packed together belowdecks. Each day their only food was a bowl of pork and beans and a cup of water.

The journey took eight weeks, and there were terrible storms. Everyone wondered if they would make it.

Finally the ship arrived safely at the Battery on the southern tip of Manhattan Island.

Mary's father found a room. It was in a dark basement on James Street in lower Manhattan. The family crowded in. It was very damp and cold, and the smell of cooking lingered all day long. Even worse, everyone had to sleep in the same bed.

Soon after, Mary's father found a job as a laborer on the docks. Her mother got work as a maid in a mansion on Fifth Avenue. Mary and Danny started school, and baby Meghan spent the day with their neighbor, Nelly O'Reilly, and her three children.

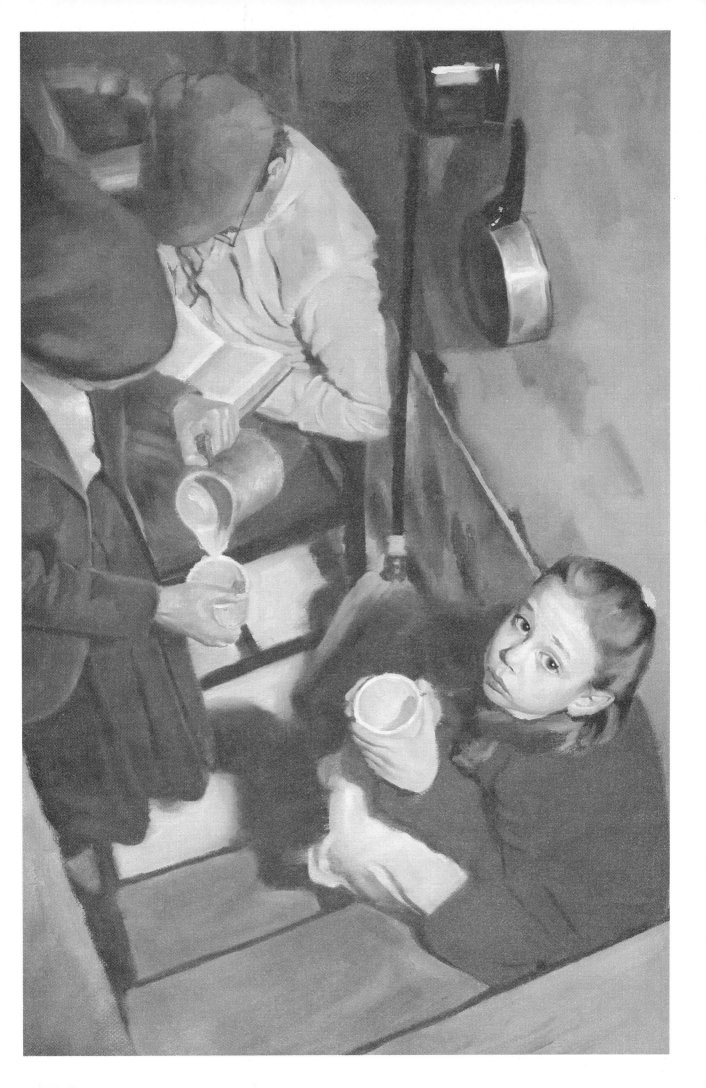

Almost everyone in the crowded basements, dug-out cellars, and tenements of James Street was Irish, and walking around after school, Mary began hearing stories. Mostly they were about the St. Patrick's Day parade on March 17th, and how grand it was and how every year Mr. Finnegan, who owned the corner grocery store, did something marvelous.

Mary really liked Mr. Finnegan. She asked Nelly O'Reilly about what he did on St. Patrick's Day.

"Oh, yes," said Nelly, rocking baby Meghan in her lap, "and it's a wonderful sight to see, girl. Mr. Finnegan has a special cart all trimmed in green and gold and a long green cloak and he rides with his dog Fergus, driving two white horses and looking like a real Irish hero. He's the most special event in the parade, and everyone here loves him for it and wouldn't miss it for the world."

Mary imagined Mr. Finnegan in his cart. The next moment, she knew that what she wanted most was to ride with him in the St. Patrick's Day parade.

The following day, she went to see him in the store. He was standing behind the counter. He didn't look like an Irish hero now. He just looked like old Mr. Finnegan. Beside him, as usual, lay Fergus, the same sleepy Irish wolfhound she had seen before.

Mary marched bravely to the counter. "Mr. Finnegan," she said, "next year I want to ride with you and Fergus in the Saint Patrick's Day parade."

Mr. Finnegan smiled. "Well now, my girl, that's a pretty steep request. No one has ever ridden with me before. You'd have to do something pretty important for me even to consider it. But let me see. If you found a perfect shamrock, I might change my mind."

Mary looked out at the icy street. Where, in all of wintry, snow-covered Manhattan, could she find a perfect shamrock?

She ran home. That night after dinner, she told her parents what Mr. Finnegan had said.

Her father settled down in their one chair. "Hmmm," he said. "Can't say I know how you'd find such a thing. Except by magic, of course."

Then he began a story of the Old Country, of a merchant and a mischievous leprechaun and how the merchant had captured the leprechaun and was about to make off with his crock of gold when he made the mistake of turning away.

"You know," said Mary's father, "you can't ever take your eyes off a leprechaun. If you do, he will escape. And that's exactly what happened to the merchant."

Mary's father was a very good storyteller, but Mary was very tired. "I'd never have let that leprechaun escape," she said as he finished. Then she fell asleep between her mother and her brother in the big bed.

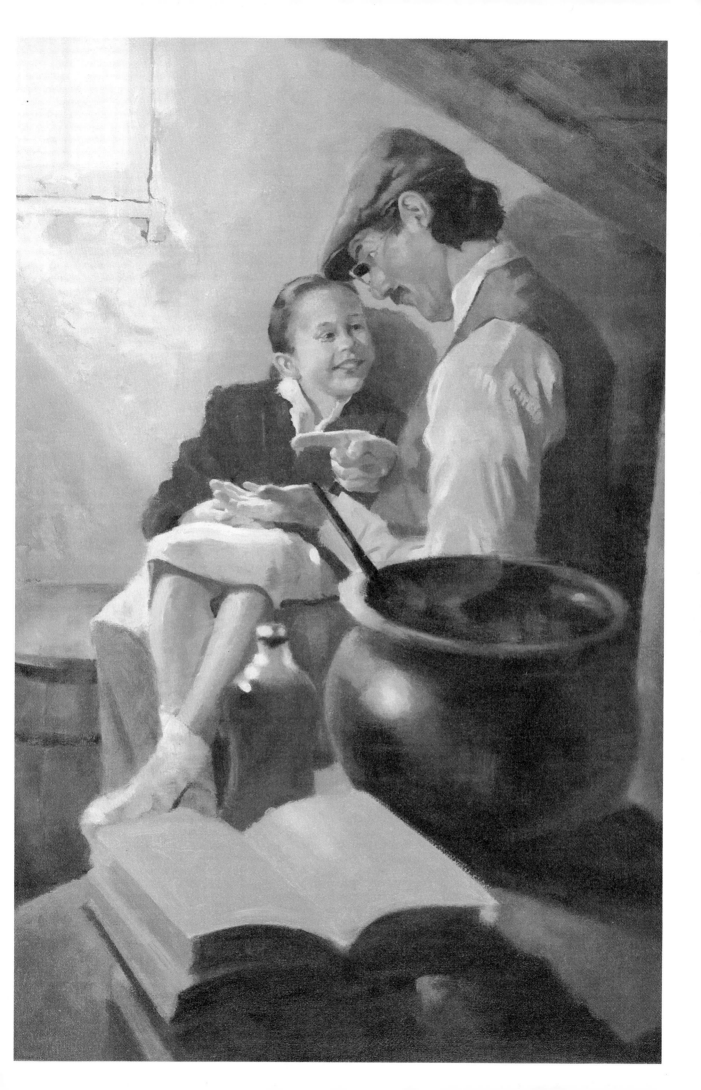

The next morning, Danny scoffed at the idea of Mary ever finding a shamrock in the snow. Two years older, he had refused to continue school and was selling newspapers with a bunch of other newsboys on Broadway. He stormed out the door, making a mean face. "You wait!" Mary shouted after him. "I'll find one!"

In the afternoon, she went down to the ferry slip on Catherine Street. She loved watching the ferries steaming to and fro on the East River. Watching them helped her to think.

Shamrocks always turned up in fields of grass. Even though it was covered in snow, there was lots of grass in City Hall Park. Surely she could find a shamrock there.

She went up Madison Street and across William and found herself in the park. There was almost no one on the paths. Mary walked all around looking at the snow. Every so often, she knelt down and dug through to the dry grass beneath. She looked and looked until the sun began going down and her back hurt. No shamrocks.

Exhausted, ready to give up, she collapsed on a bench. Just then, she heard a tap-tap-tapping nearby. She followed the noise. Crouching under a hedge near City Hall was a tiny old man in a cocked hat and a leather apron. He was tapping the heel back on his shoe with a little silver hammer.

Mary walked right over. "I thought leprechauns stayed in Ireland," she said.

The leprechaun grinned. "There are so many Irish in America now, I had to see the place. I'm going all the way to California as soon as I fix this shoe. I don't want to miss the gold rush."

Mary took a deep breath. There in his lapel was a perfect shamrock! She leaned forward. "Could you please give me that shamrock?"

"I can't," said the leprechaun. "I need it for luck in California. Why do you ask?"

Mary explained about the parade and Mr. Finnegan.

The leprechaun laughed. "I'll be on my way home in March. Maybe I'll catch that parade. Who knows? I might have the shamrock for you then." With that he finished repairing his shoe, put it on, and disappeared.

Mary walked home, puzzled. A leprechaun in America, and he might give her a shamrock? She told no one about what had happened, but for weeks afterward, she kept looking on her own. It didn't seem very wise to be depending on a leprechaun.

One day, she even got Tom, the milkman, to take her north of Forty-second Street in his wagon. There the buildings thinned out and turned into fields. She spent the whole afternoon tramping through the snow, but she didn't find a thing.

Around Christmas, to earn a little pocket money, Mary began walking Fergus. Late one afternoon, as she was leaving the store, Mr. Finnegan said, "Tough luck about the shamrock."

Mary stood very still. She nodded.

"Who knows?" said Mr. Finnegan. "Something may turn up."

Mary wasn't so sure.

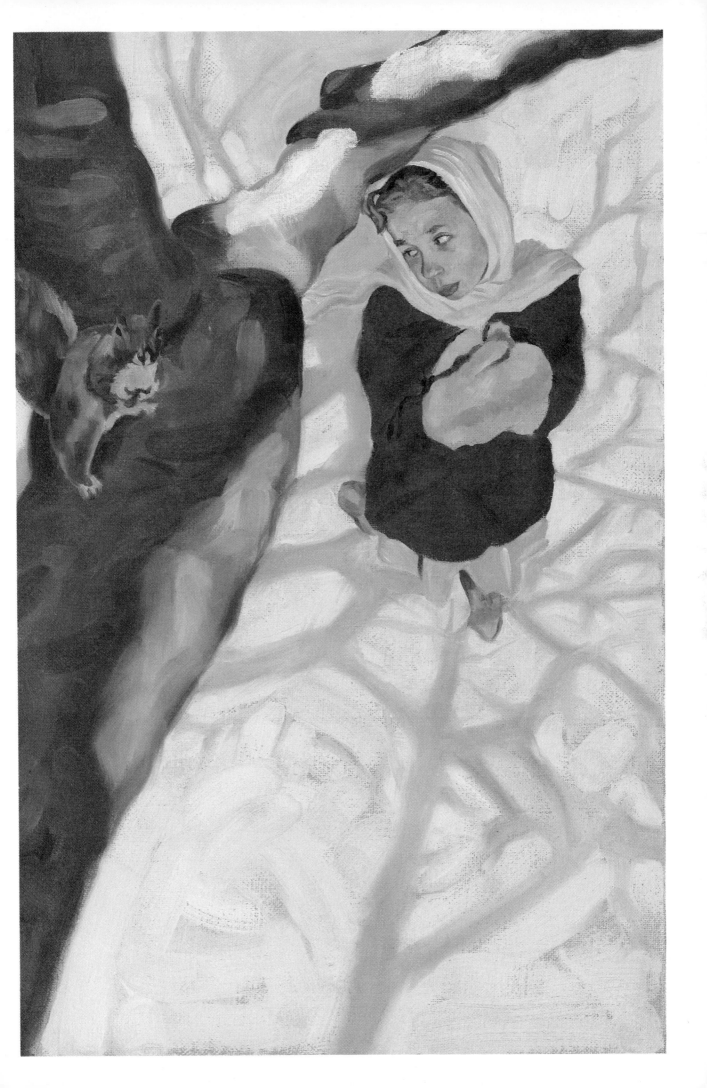

And then it was Christmas with a meal of turkey scraps, and a small doll made by her mother. The weather got so cold, they all had to huddle in bed in their clothes. But suddenly, unbelievably, it was the afternoon before St. Patrick's Day.

Mary walked Fergus to City Hall Park. She'd never find a shamrock now. That leprechaun would never turn up.

She wanted so much to be in the parade, and now she never would be. She kicked a stone along the path and suddenly, there was the leprechaun, crouching in the same spot as before. He looked a little dusty from all his travels.

He grinned. "I see you didn't forget me."

"Did you have a nice trip?" Mary asked. But then she looked at his lapel. The shamrock was gone!

Mary knew he must have it hidden. She also remembered her father's storytelling. She grabbed the leprechaun in both hands, looked right at him, and said, "Give me the shamrock or bring me to your crock of gold!"

The leprechaun's eyes grew bright. His cheeks puffed up in surprise.

"You've dropped your dog's leash!" he sputtered.

"What?" said Mary, glancing at the ground. At that moment the leprechaun wriggled free, flipped into the air past Fergus's snapping jaws, and was gone.

"Oh, no!" cried Mary. "How could I have done that?"

Dejected, with Fergus by her side, she walked back to James Street. She said nothing to Mr. Finnegan when she hung up the leash behind the door. She didn't even wish him a happy St. Patrick's Day as she started for home.

But that night, when her father came in for supper, he was smiling. Before he would even sit down, he took something out of his pocket and covered it with his other hand.

"I was walking past City Hall," he said, "and would you believe what I found behind a hedge?"

He took his other hand away. In his palm was the most perfect shamrock Mary had ever seen.

Where had it come from? Was it the leprechaun? "Oh, Daddy," Mary said.

"It's for you, daughter. You'll be able to ride with Mr. Finnegan now!"

The next day, Mary's parents took Danny and baby Meghan to the St. Patrick's Day parade on Fifth Avenue. Behind the police barricade, they listened to the bands and the sound of marching feet. There were rows and rows of policemen, and group after group carrying Irish and American flags.

And then, there was Mr. Finnegan! He was sitting in his cart, driving the two white horses. The cart was covered in the green drapery fringed with gold, and Mr. Finnegan himself was dressed in a wreath of oak leaves and his long green cloak trimmed with gold and green. Behind him, sitting on a mat, was Fergus, and beside Fergus stood Mary McLean, smiling the biggest smile anyone had ever seen.

AUTHOR'S NOTE

While all the characters and events in this story have been made up, they are based — with the exception of the leprechaun, of course — on life as it was lived by Irish immigrants in New York City in the 1850s.

Under British rule, the potato had been Ireland's principal crop. Between 1845 and 1849, a blight that spread from America caused the Great Potato Famine. The effects of the famine lasted until 1855. During that time, more than a million Irish fled to American shores. Many settled on James and Pike streets in lower Manhattan, streets that today are part of an industrial and financial district.

No one knows when the first St. Patrick's Day parade took place in America, but by the 1850s there was one in most major cities. The biggest and boldest was always in New York. The parades are part of the joyful side of a holiday that is at once festive and religious and demonstrates the pride of the Irish while celebrating the patron saint of Ireland.

Saint Patrick himself was born in the British Isles, probably near the modern city of Dumbarton, Scotland, around 385 A.D. The Roman Empire had conquered Great Britain three centuries before, and Saint Patrick's father, Calpurnius, held an important position with the Roman government. When Patrick was sixteen, he was kidnapped and sold into slavery in Ireland. Six years later he escaped and devoted himself to God. Eventually, as a bishop, he returned to convert the citizens of Ireland to Christianity. (It is said that he used the three-leaved shamrock, symbol of the green of Ireland, to teach the Trinity.)

The day that honors Saint Patrick is not his birthday but the day he died. The many myths that surround him help make his celebration even more colorful. Not even a leprechaun — that solitary, bad-tempered, shoemaking Irish fairy – could quarrel with that.

Steven Kroll